This toddler

belongs to

_____

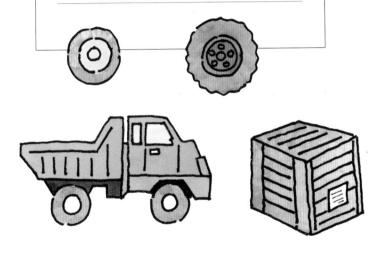

Using this book

Ladybird's toddler talkabouts are ideal for
encouraging children to talk about what they see.
Bold, colourful pictures and simple questions help
to develop early learning skills – such as matching,
counting and detailed observation.

Look at this book together. First talk about the
pictures yourself, and point out things to look at.
Let your child take her* time. With encouragement,
she will start to join in, talking about the familiar
things in the pictures. Help her to count objects,
to look for things that match, and to talk about
what is going on in the picture stories.

*To avoid the clumsy use of he/she, the child is referred to as 'she'.
Toddler talkabouts are suitable for both boys and girls.*

All Ladybird books are available at most bookshops,
supermarkets and newsagents, or can be ordered direct from:
Ladybird Postal Sales
PO Box 133 Paignton TQ3 2YP England
Telephone: (+44) 01803 554761
Fax: (+44) 01803 663394

A catalogue record for this book is available
from the British Library

Published by Ladybird Books Ltd
A subsidiary of the Penguin Group
A Pearson Company
© LADYBIRD BOOKS LTD MCMXCVIII

LADYBIRD and the device of a Ladybird are trademarks of
Ladybird Books Ltd Loughborough Leicestershire UK

I like
big trucks

illustrated by Richard Morgan
and Terry Burton

Ladybird

Look for these big trucks
when you go to town.

What colours are these trucks?

What is your favourite colour?

Count the dumper trucks.

How many red ones are there?

Look at the pictures and
tell the story.

Point to the combine harvester.

What else can you see?

Look at the building site.

Point to the cement mixer.

Match the drivers to their trucks.

Find another...

minibus

tanker

tractor

Which truck is the biggest?

What jobs do you think they do?

Match each picture to its blue shadow.

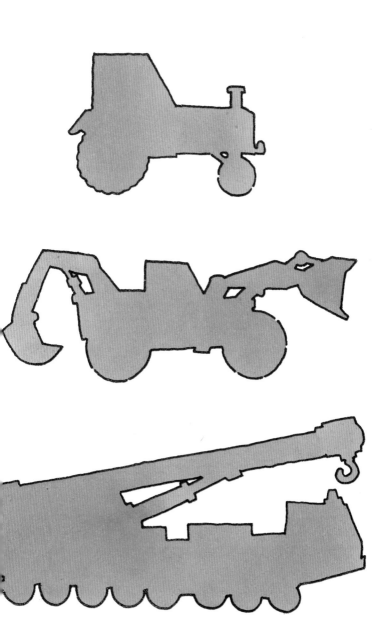

Count the lorries in each box.

What a busy building site!

Can you make the noises?